Wet Dog!

by Elise Broach

illustrations by David Catrow

SCHOLASTIC INC.
New York Toronto London Auckland Sydney
Mexico City New Delhi Hong Kong Buenos Aires

For Grace
—E.B.

To Goobie, the mustache man
—D.C.

ISBN 0-439-85651-5

12 11 10 9 8 7 6 5 4 3   6 7 8 9 10 11/0

Printed in the U.S.A.   40

First Scholastic printing, March 2006

Designed by Lily Malcom
Text set in New Hampshire
The art was created using pencil and watercolor.

*H*e was a good old dog and a hot old dog, as he lay in the noonday sun. And he dozed and he drowsed in the beating-down sun, with his long pink tongue hanging out.

Well, that too-hot dog in the too-hot sun just had to cool off somehow. So he heaved to his feet, and he sniffed the air, and he trotted off down the road . . .

pat-a-pat, pat-a-pat, pat.

And that's when he saw a man washing a car,
a long black, shiny black car.

Old dog stepped in the soft, cool stream till the wet soaked through to his skin. Then he shook and he shook with a happy-dog smile, wagging his happy-dog tail . . . shaky-shake, shaky-shake, shake!

"Wet dog!" cried the man with the shiny black car. "Shoo! Go on now, shoo!"

Wet dog smiled his sorry-dog smile and wagged his sorry-dog tail.
Then he flapped his ears, and he sniffed the air, and he trotted off
down the road . . . pat-a-pat, pat-a-pat, pat.

And that's when he saw a lady washing some pans, some piled-high, sticky-high pans.

DISH SUDZ

Wet dog stepped in the splash and the suds till the cool flowed down his fur.

Then he shook and he shook with a happy-dog smile, wagging his happy-dog tail . . .

shaky-shake, shaky-shake, shake!

"Wet dog!" cried the lady with the sticky-high pans. "Shoo! Go on now, shoo!"

Wet dog smiled his sorry-dog smile and wagged his sorry-dog tail.
Then he flapped his ears, and he sniffed the air, and he trotted off
down the road . . . pat-a-pat, pat-a-pat, pat.

And that's when he saw a lady spraying some blooms, some pale pink, petal pink blooms.

Wet dog stepped in the sparkling spray, and the soft mist cooled his face. Then he shook and he shook with a happy-dog smile, wagging his happy-dog tail . . . shaky-shake, shaky-shake, shake!

"Wet dog!" cried the lady with the petal pink blooms. "Shoo! Go on now, shoo!"

Wet dog smiled his sorry-dog smile and wagged his sorry-dog tail.
Then he flapped his ears, and he sniffed the air, and he trotted off
down the road . . . pat-a-pat, pat-a-pat, pat.

And that's when he saw some men playing a song, a singing-loud, dancing-loud song. Wet dog stood by the side of the creek, feeling the music rise.

Then he danced right into the trickle and the muck with his big, soft paws sinking in.

And he shook and he shook with a happy-dog smile, wagging his happy-dog tail . . . shaky-shake, shaky-shake, shake!

"Wet dog!" cried the men with the dancing-loud song.
"Shoo! Go on now, shoo!"

Wet dog smiled his sorry-dog smile and wagged his sorry-dog tail.
Then he flapped his ears, and he sniffed the air, and he trotted off
down the road . . . pat-a-pat, pat-a-pat, pat.

That's when he came to a lake.

Now, there by the shore in the beating-down sun were people in fine, fancy clothes. There were ladies in curls, men in bow ties, babies in soft, flouncy hats. Wet dog stood by the lake, and he looked at the crowd in the too-too-too-hot sun.

Then he stepped right into the shimmering cool of that whoo-cool, too-cool lake. And he splished and he splashed in the rippling waves, and he bounded back onto the shore.

He was wet to the bone, so he shook and he shook . . .
shaky-shake, shaky-shake, shake!

"Wet dog!" cried the people in their fine, fancy clothes.
"Shoo! Go on now, SHOOOOOOO!"

But wet dog shook with his ears flying fast, and his wet fur spray-spray-spraying.

And a baby just laughed. She was a fine, fancy baby, in too-hot clothes, with the water fresh on her face. She laughed and she laughed, clapping her hands at the wet-dog rain in the air.

"More!" cried the baby, arms open wide. "More, dog, more, dog! More!"

Then the people laughed too.

And they danced and they dove and they splashed and they strode into the blue-cool, oooo-cool water.

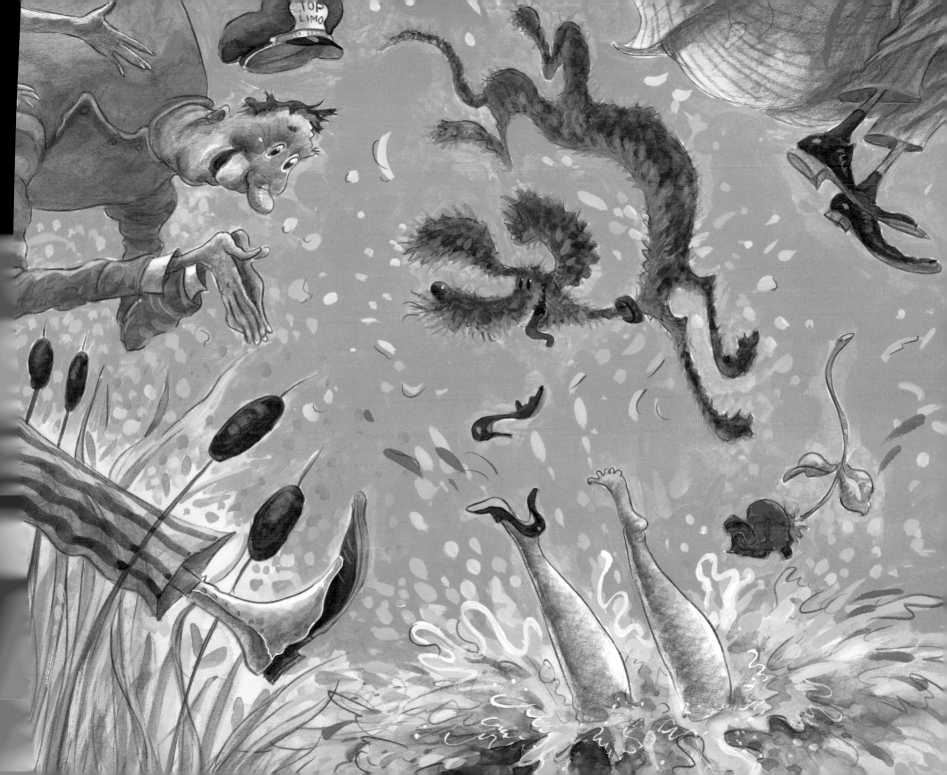

Well, they splashed and they danced—how they splashed and they danced!—as the sun slid low in the sky. And they patted wet dog from his ears to his tail . . .

"Hoo-ray, wet dog!
Hoo-ray!"

Wet Dog!

by Elise Broach • illustrations by David Catrow